Being a DOG

A Tail of Mindfulness

Words by **MARIA GIANFERRARI**
Pictures by **PETE OSWALD**

HARPER
An Imprint of HarperCollinsPublishers

To our beloved family dogs present: Maple, Luna & Barkley
And past: Becca, Elvis, Bumper, Mac, Willow, Honey, Chance,
Allie, Marble, Brandi & Dylan
—M.G.

Inspired by Radar
—P.O.

Can you be like a dog?
Being like a dog
is BE-ing.

Right now.

Not before

or after.

Just now.

Stretch while you rise.

Wag your body.

Greet the day

and everyone you love.

Munch your food.

Lap your drink.

Can you sniff like a dog?
Breathe deep.

Sniff,

sniff,

sniffing . . .

everything.

Let's play like a dog!
Invite your friends,

then romp,

race,

and chase.

Tag and tug.

Play every day.

Rain or shine.

Like a dog, feel what you're feeling:

Bark if you're worried.

Growl if you're angry.

Yowl if you're sad.

Sing if you're happy.

again

and again!

Be curious.   Feel the emotion,

then let it go
and
BE.

Let the wind ruffle your fur.

Nap in the sun

or the shade.

Wade and watch in the water.

Tunnel and shovel in the sand.

Hide and leap from the leaves!

Whirl and roll and swirl in the snow.

Take a taste.

(But not if it's yellow!)

Let's sleep like a dog:

Notice the night.

Feel the fatigue.

Circle before
you sleep.

Drop
and dream.

Let's be
like a dog
right
now.

TAKE A MINDFUL NATURE WALK WITH A FRIEND!

Find some green space, whether it's a city park or country woods.

SNIFF like a DOG

Breathe in deeply and close your eyes. Do you smell . . .

HEAR like a DOG

Close your eyes.
Listen. Do you hear . . .

SPRING

cherry blossoms?
pollen? (ah-choo!)
earthy rain?

croaking frogs?
the cracking of
baseballs on bats?
drumming woodpeckers?

Humans have around 6 million receptors for detecting smell, while dogs have over 300 million!

SUMMER

fresh-cut grass?
barbeque?
cotton candy?

swishing
jump ropes?
buzzing mosquitoes?
booming thunder
and fireworks?

FALL

cinnamon?
musky leaves?
spicy apple cider?

the whisper of fallen leaves?
acorns plopping?
honking geese?

WINTER

fresh snow?
chimney smoke?
evergreen trees?

the scritch-scratch of
ice skates?
snow crunching underfoot?
sloshing slush?

A dog's sense of
smell is so keen that
they can detect one
grain of sugar in
1,000 grains of salt!

Dogs are better at hearing
higher frequency sounds,
like the squeak of a mouse,
while the human ear
hears lower frequency
sounds better.

SEE ^{like a} DOG

Look around: up, down, over, and under.
Do you see . . .

daffodils?
robins' eggs?
bumblebees?

FEEL ^{like a} DOG

What do the things you touch feel like?
Notice all the different textures. Do you
feel . . .

sticky mud?
bumpy toads?
velvety pussy willows?

TASTE ^{like a} DOG

Yum! Do you taste . . .

strawberries and cream?
fiddleheads?
lemonade?

Dogs can't see the same colors that we do. They mostly see yellows and blues.

SUMMER

dandelions?
monarch butterflies?
bluebirds?

soft sand?
rough rocks?
smooth shells?

ice cream?
s'mores?
watermelon?

FALL

colorful leaves?
school buses?
bright blue skies?

silky milkweed seeds?
bristly pinecones?
brittle leaves?

caramel apples?
pumpkin pie?
cider donuts?

WINTER

icicles?
snowmen?
feathery frost?

itchy wool?
cozy fleece?
snowballs?

hot chocolate
with whipped cream?
candy canes?
holiday cookies?

Dogs' fur feels fluffy
and soft. Their tongues
are smooth and wet.
Their ears are like velour.
Ouch! Don't forget
that whoosh of
a wagging tail!

Dogs only have
about 1,700 taste buds.
Humans have 9,000!

MINDFUL BREATHING EXERCISE

We like to feel happy, but it's hard to feel sad and scared. When we're feeling this way, it helps to first notice that feeling and greet it like it's a friend: "Hello, sadness. How are you doing today?" or "Greetings, fear. I see you're here again." Feel the emotion—hold it like a kite, and then let it fly away. One thing that can help when we're feeling sad and scared is breathing deeply.

- 🐾 Sit still.
- 🐾 Close your eyes.
- 🐾 Imagine that your lungs are like a big balloon that you're filling with air.
- 🐾 Slowly count to five as you breathe in: one, two, three, four five. In your mind, see the balloon fill up with air.
- 🐾 Hold it for a moment. See the full balloon. Then slowly breathe out, counting backward, five, four, three, two, one, as you see the balloon get smaller and smaller.

Repeat this three times and several times a day.

Deep breathing gets more oxygen to your brain and will help you feel calmer.